Tcheriapin

Sax Rohmer

Table of Contents

Tcheriapin...**1**

   Sax Rohmer...1

   1. THE ROSE...2

   THE STRANGER'S STORY...6

   2. "THE BLACK MASS"..16

Tcheriapin

Sax Rohmer

- 1. THE ROSE
- THE STRANGER'S STORY
- 2. "THE BLACK MASS"

Tcheriapin

1. THE ROSE

Examine it closely," said the man in the unusual caped overcoat. "It will repay examination."

I held the little object in the palm of my hand, bending forward over the marble-topped table and looking down at it with deep curiosity. The babel of tongues so characteristic of Malay Jack's, and that mingled odour of stale spirits, greasy humanity, tobacco, cheap perfume, and opium, which distinguishes the establishment, faded from my ken. A sense of loneliness came to me.

Perhaps I should say that it became complete. I had grown conscious of its approach at the very moment that the cadaverous white-haired man had addressed me. There was a quality in his steadfast gaze and in his oddly pitched deep voice which from the first had wrapped me about— as though he were cloaking me in his queer personality and withdrawing me from the common plane.

Having stared for some moments at the object in my palm, I touched it gingerly; whereupon my acquaintance laughed—a short bass laugh.

"It looks fragile," he said. "But have no fear. It is nearly as hard as a diamond."

Thus encouraged, I took the thing up between finger and thumb, and held it before my eyes.

For long enough I looked at it, and looking, my wonder grew.

I thought that here was the most wonderful example of the lapidary's art which I had ever met with, East or West.

It was a tiny pink rose, no larger than the nail of my little finger. Stalk and leaves were there, and golden pollen lay in its delicate heart. Each fairy-petal blushed with June fire; the frail leaves were exquisitely green. Withal it was as hard and unbendable as a thing of steel.

2

Tcheriapin

"Allow me," said the masterful voice.

A powerful lens was passed by my acquaintance. I regarded the rose through the glass, and thereupon I knew, beyond doubt, that there was something phenomenal about the gem—if gem it were. I could plainly trace the veins and texture of every petal.

I suppose I looked somewhat startled. Although, baldly stated, the fact may not seem calculated to affrighten, in reality there was something so weird about this unnatural bloom that I dropped it on the table. As I did so I uttered an exclamation; for in spite of the stranger's assurances on the point, I had by no means overcome my idea of the thing's fragility.

"Don't be alarmed," he said, meeting my startled gaze. "It would need a steam—hammer to do any serious damage."

He replaced the jewel in his pocket, and when I returned the lens to him he acknowledged it with a grave inclination of the head. As I looked into his sunken eyes, in which I thought lay a sort of sardonic merriment, the fantastic idea flashed through my mind that I had fallen into the clutches of an expert hypnotist who was amusing himself at my expense; that the miniature rose was a mere hallucination produced by the same means as the notorious Indian rope trick..Then, looking around me at the cosmopolitan groups surrounding the many tables, and catching snatches of conversations dealing with subjects so diverse as the quality of whisky in Singapore, the frail beauty of Chinese maidens, and the ways of "bloody greasers," common sense reasserted itself.

I looked into the grey face of my acquaintance.

"I cannot believe," I said slowly, "that human ingenuity could so closely duplicate the handiwork of nature. Surely the gem is unique?—possibly one of those magical talismans of which we read in Eastern stories?"

' My companion smiled.

"It is not a gem," he replied, "and whilst in a sense it is a product of human ingenuity, it is also the handiwork of nature."

3

Tcheriapin

I was badly puzzled, and doubtless revealed the fact, for the stranger laughed in his short fashion, and:

"I am not trying to mystify you," he assured me. "But the truth is so hard to believe sometimes that in the present case I hesitate to divulge it. Did you ever meet Tchériapin?"

This abrupt change of topic somewhat startled me, but nevertheless:

"I once heard him play," I replied. "Why do you ask the question?"

"For this reason: Tchériapin possessed the only other example of this art which so far as I am aware ever left the laboratory of the inventor. He occasionally wore it in his buttonhole."

"It is then a manufactured product of some sort?"

"As I have said, in a sense it is; but"—he drew the tiny exquisite ornament from his pocket again and held it up before me—"it is a natural bloom."

"What?"

"It is a natural bloom," replied my acquaintance, fixing his penetrating gaze upon me. "By a perfectly simple process invented by the cleverest chemist of his age it has been reduced to this gem–like state whilst retaining unimpaired every one of its natural beauties, every shade of its natural colour. You are incredulous?"

"On the contrary," I replied, "having examined it through a magnifying glass I had already assured myself that no human hand had fashioned it. You arouse my curiosity intensely. Such a process, with its endless possibilities, should be worth a fortune to the inventor."

The stranger nodded grimly and again concealed the rose in his pocket.

"You are right," he said; "and the secret died with the man who discovered it—in the great explosion at the Vortex Works in 1917. You recall it? The T N T. factory? It shook all London, and fragments were cast into three counties."

4

Tcheriapin

"I recall it perfectly well."

"You remember also the death of Dr. Kreener, the chief chemist? He died in an endeavor to save some of the work–people."

"I remember."

"He was the inventor of the process, but it was never put upon the market. He was a singular man, sir; as was once said of him: 'A Don Juan of science.' Dame Nature gave him her heart unwooed. He trifled with science as some men trifle with love, tossing aside with a smile discoveries which would have made another famous. This"—tapping his breast pocket—"was one of them."

"You astound me. Do I understand you to mean that Dr. Kreener had invented a process for reducing any form of plant life to this condition?"

"Almost any form," was the guarded reply. "And some forms of animal life."

"What!"

"If you like"—the stranger leaned forward and grasped my arm—"I will tell you the story of Dr. Kreener's last experiment."

I was now intensely interested. I had not forgotten the heroic death of the man concerning whose work this chance acquaintance of mine seemed to know so much. And in the cadaverous face of the stranger as he sat there regarding me fixedly there was a promise and an allurement. I stood on the verge of strange things; so that, looking into the deep–set eyes, once again I felt the cloak being drawn about me, and I resigned myself willingly to the illusion.

From the moment when he began to speak again until that when I rose and followed him from Malay Jack's, as I shall presently relate, I became oblivious of my surroundings. I lived and moved through those last fevered hours in the lives of Dr. Kreener, Tchériapin, the violinist, and that other tragic figure around whom the story centered. I append:

Tcheriapin

THE STRANGER'S STORY

I asked you (said the man in the caped coat) if you had ever seen Tchériapin, and you replied that you had once heard him play. Having once heard him play you will not have forgotten him. At that time, although war still raged, all musical London was asking where he had come from, and to what nation he belonged. Then when he disappeared it was variously reported, you will recall, that he had been shot as a spy and that he had escaped from England and was serving with the Austrian army. As to his parentage I can enlighten you in a measure. He was an Eurasian. His father was an aristocratic Chinaman, and his mother a Polish ballet–dancer—that was his parentage; but I would scarcely hesitate to affirm that he came from Hell; and I shall presently show you that he has certainly returned there.

You remember the strange stories current about him. The cunning ones said that he had a clever press agent. This was true enough. One of the most prominent agents in London discovered him playing in a Paris cabaret. Two months later he was playing at the Queen's Hall, and musical London lay at his feet.

He had something of the personality of Paganini, as you remember, except that he was a smaller man; long, gaunt, yellowish hands and the face of a haggard Mephistopheles. The critics quarrelled about him, as critics only quarrel about real genius, and whilst one school proclaimed that Tchériapin had discovered an entirely new technique, a revolutionary system of violin playing, another school was equally positive in declaring that he could not play at all, that he was a mountebank, a trickster, whose proper place was in a variety theatre.

There were stories, too, that were never published—not only about Tchériapin, but concerning the Strad upon which he played. If all this atmosphere of mystery which surrounded the man had truly been the work of a press agent, then the agent must have been as great a genius as his client.

But I can assure you that the stories concerning Tchériapin, true and absurd alike, were not inspired for business purposes; they grew up around him like fungi.

I can see him now, a lean, almost emaciated figure, with slow, sinuous movements, and a trick of glancing sideways with those dark, unfathomable, slightly oblique eyes. He could take up his bow in such a way as to create an atmosphere of electrical suspense. He was loathsome, yet fascinating. One's mental attitude towards him was one of defence, of being tensely on guard.

Then he would play..You have heard him play, and it is therefore unnecessary for me to attempt to describe the effect of that music. The only composition which ever bore his name—I refer to "The Black Mass"—affected me on every occasion when I heard it, as no other composition has ever done.

Perhaps it was Tchériapin's playing rather than the music itself which reached down into hitherto unplumbed depths within me, and awakened dark things which, unsuspected, lay there sleeping. I never heard "The Black Mass" played by anyone else; indeed, I am not aware that it was ever published. But had it been we should rarely hear it. Like Locke's music to Macbeth it bears an unpleasant reputation; to include it in any concert programme would be to court disaster. An idle superstition, perhaps, but there is much naïveté in the artistic temperament.

Men detested Tchériapin, yet when he chose he could win over his bitterest enemies. Women followed him as children followed the Pied Piper; he courted none, but was courted by all. He would glance aside with those black, slanting eyes, shrug in his insolent fashion, and turn away.

And they would follow. God knows how many of them followed—whether through the dens of Limehouse or the more fashionable salons of vice in the West End—they followed—perhaps down to Hell. So much for Tchétiapin.

At the lime when the episode occurred to which I have referred, Dr. Kreener occupied a house in Regent's Park, to which, when his duties at the munition works allowed, he would sometimes retire at week–ends. He was a man of complex personality. I think no one ever knew him thoroughly; indeed, I doubt if he knew himself.

He was hail–fellow–well–met with the painters, sculptors, poets and social reformers who have made of Soho a new Mecca. No movement in art was so modern that Dr. Kreener was not conversant with it; no development in Bolshevism so violent or so secret that Dr. Kreener could not speak of it complacently and with inside knowledge.

Tcheriapin

These were his Bohemian friends, these dreamers and schemers. Of this side of his life his scientific colleagues knew little or nothing, but in his hours of leisure at Regent's Park it was with these dreamers that he loved to surround himself rather than with his brethren of the laboratory. I think if Dr. Kreener had not been a great chemist he would have been a great painter, or perhaps a politician, or even a poet. Triumph was his birthright, and the fruits for which lesser men reached out in vain fell ripe into his hands.

The favourite meeting–place for these oddly assorted boon companions was the doctor's laboratory, which was divided from the house by a moderately large garden. Here on a Sunday evening one might meet the very "latest" composer, the sculptor bringing a new "message," or the man destined to supplant with the ballet the time–worn operatic tradition.

But whilst some of these would come and go, so that one could never count with certainty upon meeting them, there was one who never failed to be present when such an informal reception was held. Of him I must speak at greater length, for a reason which will shortly appear.

Andrews was the name by which he was known to the circles in which he moved. No one, from Sir John Tennier, the fashionable portrait painter, to Kruski, of the Russian ballet, disputed Andrews's right to be counted one of the elect. Yet it was known, nor did he trouble to hide the fact, that Andrews was employed at a large printing works in South London, designing advertise–ments.

He was a great, red–bearded, unkempt Scotsman, and only once can I remember to have seen him strictly sober; but to hear him talk about painters and painting in his thick Caledonian accent was to look into the soul of an artist.

He was as sour as an unripe grape–fruit, cynical, embittered, a man savagely disappointed with life and the world; and tragedy was written all over him. If anyone knew the secret of his wasted life it was Dr. Kreener, and Dr. Kreener was a reliquary of so many secrets that this one was safe as if the grave had swallowed it.

One Sunday Tchériapin joined the party. That he would gravitate there sooner or later was inevitable, for the laboratory in the garden was a kaaba to which all such spirits made at least one pilgrimage. He had just set musical London on fire with his barbaric playing,

8

Tcheriapin

and already those stories to which I have referred were creeping into circulation.

Although Dr. Kreener never expected anything of his guests beyond an interchange of ideas, it was a fact that the laboratory contained an almost unique collection of pencil and charcoal studies by famous artists, done upon the spot; of statuettes in wax, putty, soap, and other extemporized materials, by the newest sculptors. Whilst often enough from the drawing-room which opened upon the other end of the garden had issued the strains of masterly piano-playing, and it was no uncommon thing for little groups to gather in the neighbouring road to listen, gratis, to the voice of some great vocalist.

From the first moment of their meeting an intense antagonism sprang up between Tchériapin and Andrews. Neither troubled very much to veil it. In Tchériapin it found expression in covert sneers and sidelong glances, whilst the big, lion-maned Scotsman snorted open contempt of the Eurasian violinist. However, what I was about to say was that Tchériapin on the occasion of his first visit brought his violin.

It was there, amid those incongruous surroundings, that I first had my spirit tortured by the strains of "The Black Mass."

There were five of us present, including Tchériapin, and not one of the four listeners was unaffected by the music. But the influence which it exercised upon Andrews was so extraordinary as almost to reach the phenomenal. He literally writhed in his chair, and finally interrupted the performance by staggering rather than walking out of the laboratory.

I remember that he upset a jar of acid in his stumbling exit. It flowed across the floor almost to the feet of Tchériapin, and the way in which the little blackhaired man skipped, squealing, out of the path of the corroding fluid was curiously like that of a startled rabbit. Order was restored in due course, but we could not induce Tchériapin to play again, nor did Andrews return until the violinist had taken his departure. We found him in the dining-room, a nearly empty whisky-bottle beside him, and:

"I had to gang awa'," he explained thickly; "he was temptin' me to murder him. I should ha'
had to do it if I had stayed. Damn his hell-music."

Tcheriapin

Tchériapin revisited Dr. Kreener on many occasions afterwards, although for a long time he did not bring his violin again. The doctor had prevailed upon Andrews to tolerate the Eurasian's company, and I could not help noticing how Tchériapin skilfully and deliberately goaded the Scotsman, seeming to take a fiendish delight in disagreeing with his pet theories, and in discussing any topic which he had found to be distasteful to Andrews.

Chief among these was that sort of irreverent criticism of women in which male parties so often indulge. Bitter cynic though he was, women were sacred to Andrews. To speak disrespectfully of a woman in his presence was like uttering blasphemy in the study of a cardinal.

Tchériapin very quickly detected the Scotman's weakness, and one night he launched out into a series of amorous adventures which set Andrews writhing as he had writhed under the torture of "The Black Mass."

On this occasion the party was only a small one, comprising myself, Dr. Kreener, Andrews, and Tchériapin. I could feel the storm brewing, but was powerless to check it. How presently it was to break in tragic violence I could not foresee. Fate had not meant that I should foresee it..Allowing for the free play of an extravagant artistic mind, Tchériapin's career on his own showing had been that of a callous blackguard. I began by being disgusted and ended by being fascinated, not by the man's scandalous adventures, but by the scarcely human psychology of the narrator.

From Warsaw to Budapesth, Shanghai to Paris, and Cairo to London, he passed, leaving ruin behind him with a smile—airily flicking cigarette ash upon the floor to indicate the termination of each "episode."

Andrews watched him in a lowering way which I did not like at all. He had ceased to snort his scorn; indeed, for ten minutes or so he had uttered no word or sound; but there was something in the pose of his ungainly body which strangely suggested that of a great dog preparing to spring.

Presently the violinist recalled what he termed a "charming idyll of Normandy."

Tcheriapin

'There is one poor fool in the world," he said, shrugging his slight shoulders, "who never knew how badly he should hate me. Ha! ha! of him I shall tell you. Do you remember, my friends, some few years ago, a picture that was published in Paris and London? Everybody bought it; everyone said: 'He is a made man, this fellow who can paint so fine.' "

"To what picture do you refer?" asked Dr. Kreener.

"It was called 'A Dream at Dawn.' "

As he spoke the words I saw Andrews start forward, and Dr. Kreener exchanged a swift glance with him. But the Scotsman, unseen by the vainglorious half-caste, shook his head fiercely.

The picture to which Tchériapin referred will, of course, be perfectly familiar to you. It had phenomenal popularity some eight years ago. Nothing was known of the painter—whose name was Colquhoun—and nothing has been seen of his work since. The original painting was never sold, and after a time this promising new artist was, of course, forgotten.

Presently Tchériapin continued:

"It is the figure of a slender girl—ah! angels of grace!—what a girl!" He kissed his hand rapturously. "She is posed bending gracefully forward, and looking down at her own lovely reflection in the water. It is a seashore, you remember, and the little ripples play about her ankles. The first blush of the dawn robes her white body in a transparent mantle of light. Ah!

God's mercy! it was as she stood so, in a little cove of Normandy, that I saw her!"

He paused, rolling his dark eyes; and I could hear Andrews's heavy breathing; then:

"It was the 'new art'—the posing of the model not in a lighted studio, but in the scene to be depicted. And the fellow who painted her!—the man with the barbarous name! Bah! he was big—as big as our Mr. Andrews—and ugly— pooh! uglier than he! A moon-face, with cropped skull like a prize-fighter and no soul. But yes, he could paint.

11

Tcheriapin

'A Dream at Dawn' was genius— yes, some soul he must have had."

"He could paint, dear friends, but he could not love. Him I counted as—puff!"

He blew imaginary down into space.

"Her I sought out, and presently found. She told me, in those sweet stolen rambles along the shore, when the moonlight made her look like a Madonna, that she was his inspiration—his art— his life. And she wept; she wept, and I kissed her tears away.

"To please her I waited until 'A Dream at Dawn' was finished. With the finish of the picture, finished also his dream of dawn—the moon–faced one's."

Tchériapin laughed, and lighted a fresh cigarette.

"Can you believe that a man could be so stupid? He never knew of my existence, this big, red booby. He never knew that I existed until—until 'his dream' had fled—with me! In a week we were in Paris, that dream–girl and I—in a month we had quarrelled. I always end these matters with a quarrel; it makes the complete finish. She struck me in the face—and I laughed. She turned and went away. We were tired of one another.

"Ah!" Again he airily kissed his hand. "There were others after I had gone. I heard for a time.

But her memory is like a rose, fresh and fair and sweet. I am glad I can remember her so, and not as she afterwards became. That is the art of love. She killed herself with absinthe, my friends.

She died in Marseilles in the first year of the great war."

Thus far Tchériapin had proceeded, and was in the act of airily flicking ash upon the floor, when, uttering a sound which I can only describe as a roar, Andrews hurled himself upon the smiling violinist.

His great red hands clutching Tchériapin's throat, the insane Scotsman, for insane he was at that moment, forced the other back upon the settee from which he had half arisen. In

Tcheriapin

vain I sought to drag him away from the writhing body, but I doubt if any man could have relaxed that deadly grip. Tchériapin's eyes protruded hideously and his tongue lolled forth from his mouth.

One could bear the breath whistling through his nostrils as Andrews silently, deliberately, squeezed the life out of him.

It all occupied only a few minutes, and then Andrews, slowly opening his rigidly crooked fingers, stood panting and looking down at the distorted face of the dead man.

For once in his life the Scotsman was sober, and turning to Dr. Kreener:

"I have waited seven long years for this," he said, "and I'll hang wi' contentment."

I can never forget the ensuing moments, in which, amid a horrible silence only broken by the ticking of a clock, and the heavy breathing of Colquhoun (so long known to us as Andrews) we stood watching the contorted body on the settee.

And as we watched, slowly the rigid limbs began to relax, and Tchériapin slid gently on to the floor, collapsing there with a soft thud, where he squatted like some hideous Buddha, resting back against the cushions, one spectral yellow hand upraised, the fingers still clutching a big gold tassel.

Andrews (for so I always think of him) was seized with a violent fit of trembling, and he dropped into the chair from which he had made that dreadful spring, muttering to himself and looking down wild-eyed at his twitching fingers. Then he began to laugh, high-pitched laughter, in little short peals.

"Here!" cried the doctor sharply. "Drop that!"

Crossing to Andrews he grasped him by the shoulders and shook him roughly.

The laughter ceased, and— "Send for the police," said Andrews in a queer, shaky voice. "Dinna fear but I'm ready. I'm only sorry it happened here."

"You ought to be glad," said Dr. Kreener.

13

Tcheriapin

There was a covert meaning in the words—a fact which penetrated even to the dulled intelligence of the Scotsman, for he glanced up haggardly at his friend.

"You ought to be glad," repeated Dr. Kreener.

Turning, he walked to the laboratory door and locked it. He next lowered all the blinds.

"I pray that we have not been overlooked," he said, "but we must chance it." He mixed a drink for Andrews and himself. His quiet decisive manner had had its effect, and Andrews was now more composed. Indeed, he seemed to be in a half–dazed condition; but he persistently kept his back turned to the crouching figure propped up against the settee.

"If you think you can follow me," said Dr. Kreener abruptly, "I will show you the result of a recent experiment.".Unlocking a cupboard he took out a tiny figure some two inches long by one inch high, mounted upon a polished wooden pedestal. It was that of a guinea–pig. The flaky fur gleamed like the finest silk, and one felt that the coat of the minute creature would be as floss to the touch; whereas in reality it possessed the rigidity of steel. Literally one could have done it little damage with a hammer. Its weight was extraordinary.

"I am learning new things about this process every day," continued Dr. Kreener, placing the little figure upon a table. "For instance, whilst it seems to operate uniformly upon vegetable matter, there are curious modifications where one applies it to animal and mineral substances. I have now definitely decided that the result of this particular enquiry must never be published.

You, Colquhoun, I believe, possess an example of the process, a tiger lily, I think? I must ask you to return it to me. Our late friend, Tchériapin, wears a pink rose in his coat which I have treated in the same way. I am going to take the liberty of removing it."

He spoke in the hard, incisive manner which I had heard him use in the lecture theatre, and it was evident enough that his design was to prepare Andrews for something which he contemplated. Facing the Scotsman where he sat hunched up in tlie big armchair, dully watching the speaker:

Tcheriapin

"There is one experiment," said Dr. Kreener, speaking very deliberately, "which I have never before had a suitable opportunity of attempting. Of its result I am personally confident, but science always demands proof."

His voice rang now with a note of repressed excitement. He paused for a moment, and then:

"If you were to examine this little specimen very closely," he said, and rested his finger upon the tiny figure of the guinea-pig, "you would find that in one particular it is imperfect. Although a diamond drill would have to be employed to demonstrate the fact, the animal's organs, despite their having undergone a chemical change quite new to science, are intact, perfect down to the smallest detail. One part of the creature's structure alone defied my process. In short, dental enamel is impervious to it. This little animal, otherwise as complete as when it lived and breathed, has no teeth. I found it necessary to extract them before submitting the body to the reductionary process."

He paused.

"Shall I go on?" he asked.

Andrews, to whose mind, I think, no conception of the doctor's project had yet penetrated, shuddered, but slowly nodded his head.

Dr. Kreener glanced across the laboratory at the crouching figure of Tchériapin, then, resting his hands upon Andrews's shoulders, he pushed him back in the chair and stared into his dull eyes.

"Brace yourself, Colquhoun," he said tersely.

Turning, he crossed to a small mahogany cabinet at the farther end of the room. Pulling out a glass tray he judicially selected a pair of dental forceps.

15

2. "THE BLACK MASS"

Thus far the stranger's appalling story had progressed when that singular cloak in which hypnotically he had enwrapped me seemed to drop, and I found myself clutching the edge of the table and staring into the grey face of the speaker..I became suddenly aware of the babel of voices about me, of the noisome smell of Malay Jack's, and of the presence of Jack in person, who was enquiring if there were any further orders.

I was conscious of nausea.

"Excuse me," I said, rising unsteadily, "but I fear the oppressive atmosphere is affecting me."

"If you prefer to go out," said my acquaintance, in that deep voice which throughout the dreadful story had rendered me oblivious of my surroundings, "I should be much favoured if you would accompany me to a spot not five hundred yards from here."

Seeing me hesitate:

"I have a particular reason for asking," he added.

"Very well," I replied, inclining my head, "if you wish it. But certainly I must seek the fresh air."

Going up the steps and out through the door above which the blue lantern burned, we came to the street, turned to the left, to the left again, and soon were threading that maze of narrow ways which complicates the map of Pennyfields.

I felt somewhat recovered. Here, in the narrow but familiar highways the spell of my singular acquaintance lost much of its potency, and I already found myself doubting the story of Dr.

Kreener and Tchériapin. Indeed, I began to laugh at myself, conceiving that I had fallen into the hands of some comedian who was making sport of me; although why such a person should visit Malay Jack's was not apparent.

16

Tcheriapin

I was about to give expression to these new and saner ideas when my companion paused before a door half hidden in a little alley which divided the back of a Chinese restaurant from the tawdry–looking establishment of a cigar merchant. He apparently held the key, for although I did not actually hear the turning of the lock I saw that he had opened the door.

"May I request you to follow me?" came his deep voice out of the darkness. "I will show you something which will repay your trouble."

Again the cloak touched me, but it was without entirely resigning myself to the compelling influence that I followed my mysterious acquaintance up an uncarpeted and nearly dark stair. On the landing above a gas lamp was burning, and opening a door immediately facing the stair the stranger conducted me into a barely furnished and untidy room.

The atmosphere smelled like that of a pot–house, the odours of stale spirits and of tobacco mingling unpleasantly. As my guide removed his hat and stood there, a square, gaunt figure in his queer, caped overcoat, I secured for the first time a view of his face in profile; and found it to be startlingly unfamiliar. Seen thus, my acquaintance was another man. I realized that there was something unnatural about the long, white hair, the grey face; that the sharp outline of brow, nose and chin was that of a much younger man than I had supposed him to be.

All this came to me in a momentary flash of perception, for immediately my attention was riveted upon a figure hunched up on a dilapidated sofa on the opposite side of the room. It was that of a big man, bearded and very heavily built, but whose face was scarred as by years of suffering, and whose eyes confirmed the story indicated by the smell of stale spirits with which the air of the room was laden. A nearly empty bottle stood on a table at his elbow, a glass beside it, and a pipe lay in a saucer full of ashes near the glass.

As we entered, the glazed eyes of the man opened widely and he clutched at the table with big red hands, leaning forward and staring horribly.

Saving this derelict figure and some few dirty utensils and scattered garments which indicated that the apartment was used both as a sleeping and living room, there was so

17

Tcheriapin

little of interest in the place that automatically my wandering gaze strayed from the figure on the sofa to a large oil painting, unframed, which rested upon the mantelpiece above the dirty grate, in which the fire had become extinguished.

I uttered a stifled exclamation. It was "A Dream at Dawn"—evidently the original painting!

On the left of it, from a nail in the wall, hung a violin and bow, and on the right stood a sort of cylindrical glass case or closed jar upon a wooden base.

From the moment that I perceived the contents of this glass case a sense of fantasy claimed me, and I ceased to know where reality ended and mirage began.

It contained a tiny and perfect figure of a man. He was arrayed in a beautifully fitting dress–suit such as a doll might have worn, and he was posed as if in the act of playing a violin, although no violin was present. At the elfin black hair and Mephistophelian face of this horrible, wonderful image, I stared fascinatedly.

I looked and looked at the dwarfed figure of . . . Tchériapin!

All these impressions came to me in the space of a few hectic moments, when in upon my mental tumult intruded a husky whisper from the man on the sofa.

"Kreener!" he said. "Kreener!"

At the sound of that name, and because of the way in which it was pronounced, I felt my blood running cold. The speaker was staring straight at my companion.

I clutched at the open door. I felt that there was still some crowning horror to come. I wanted to escape from that reeking room, but my muscles refused to obey me, and there I stood whilst:

"Kreenerl" repeated the husky voice, and I saw that the speaker was rising unsteadily to his feet. "You have brought him again. Why have you brought him again? He will play. He will play me a step nearer to Hell!"

Tcheriapin

"Brace yourself, Colquhoun," said the voice of my companion. "Brace yourself."

"Take him awa'!" came in a sudden frenzied shriek. "Take him awa'! He's there at your elbow, Kreener, mockin' me, and pointing to that damned violin."

"Here!" said the stranger, a high note of command in his voice. "Drop that! Sit down at once."

Even as the other obeyed him, the cloaked stranger, stepping to the mantelpiece, opened a small box which lay there beside the glass case. He turned to me; and I tried to shrink away from him. For I knew—I knew—yet I loathed to look upon—what was in the box. Muffled as though reaching me through fog, I heard the words:

"A perfect human body. . . in miniature. . . every organ intact by means of . . . process . . . rendered indestructible. Tchériapin as he was in life may be seen by the curious, ten thousand years hence. Incomplete . . . one respect . . . here in this box. . ."

The spell was broken by a horrifying shriek from the man whom my companion had addressed as Colquhoun, and whom I could only suppose to be the painter of the celebrated picture which rested upon the mantelshelf.

"Take him awa', Kreener! He is reaching for the violin!"

Animation returned to me, and I fell rather than ran down the darkened stair. How I opened the street door I know not, but even as I stepped out into the squalid alleys of Pennyfields the cloaked figure was beside me. A hand was laid upon my shoulder.

"Listen!" commanded a deep voice.

Clearly, with an eerie sweetness, an evil, hellish beauty indescribable, the wailing of a Stradivarius violin crept to my ears from the room above. Slowly—slowly the music began, and my soul rose up in revolt.

"Listen!" repeated the voice. "Listen! It is 'The Black Mass'!"

Lightning Source UK Ltd.
Milton Keynes UK
UKOW022102090712

195720UK00004B/42/P

9 781162 686905